This Book Belongs To:

The Be Good Fairy

Missy Wallen-Nichols

Illustrations by Ben Ballard

Text and Illustrations Copyright © 2012 by Mawco Publishing

ISBN 978-0-9853523-0-1
Library of Congress Control Number: 2012955096

ACKNOWLEDGMENTS

A great big thank you is in order for friends, families, and colleagues that helped make our dream a published work. This book is dedicated to my loving and supportive family: Mom, Dad, Brian, and Addison.

The Be Good Fairy

Written by Missy Wallen-Nichols
Illustrations by Ben Ballard

Introduction

The Be Good Fairy is magical. No one has ever seen him or her, and for that matter, no one really knows if the fairy is a boy or girl!

The Be Good Fairy only communicates with adults, and always seems to appear exactly when needed.
On the day before the Be Good Fairy visits a home, the adults have the bright and beautiful experience of seeing fairy stardust in amazing colors to remind them that it is near. When this happens, they will be watching their children closely, so they can work on their most difficult issues.

Children then hang their "been good" sign on the door so the Be Good Fairy will know that the child has been working hard to be good.
Don't be fooled...just because you leave out your sign doesn't mean the Be Good Fairy will come.
Never forget, the Be Good Fairy is always watching...good or bad!

If you've been good, the Be Good Fairy will leave a surprise.

The Be Good Fairy always seemed to know exactly what our son wished for.
Whether it was a pack of his favorite gum, a quarter for the toy machine at the grocery store, or a new toy car,
he was excited to be rewarded for working so hard on difficult issues.

On occasion, the challenges were too much, and the Be Good Fairy chose to pass our house by.
These times made our son more determined to work harder in the future.

We journal the Be Good Fairy's visits and the surprises left along the way. This motivation helps us deal with life's little growing pains.
When things get a little overwhelming, fairy dust falls back into our lives and gives us a much needed motivational push.

This book gives fun examples of how the Be Good Fairy has helped children all over the world.
Whatever the problem may be, from potty training to going to bed on time, the Be Good Fairy will be there when needed.
So open your hearts and imaginations, and get ready to change your lives forever.

Be good, for the Be Good Fairy is watching!

Table of Contents

Bailee Goes Potty

It was a tough day at work for Bailee's dear dad.
He was tired and decided to nap just a tad.

When all of the sudden across his computer screen
spread a sea of gold stardust
with a border of bright green.

He reached for his phone
as fast as he could
to call home with the news,
"Bailee, be good!"

He had to tell Bailee the news of the day. "Be sure to go potty," he was quick to say.
"Where did she go?" Bailee's mom peeks to see. What a surprise...Bailee went pee!

What a big girl Bailee was
on the potty big and tall,
with thoughts of the Be Good Fairy
and a new lovable doll.

Before going to bed, she hung her sign on the knob
to let the Be Good Fairy know she had done a great job.

When morning came, she could hardly wait.
She ran into the hall to find out her fate.
Outside she could see, with great joy on her face,
a beautiful doll appeared without a trace!

3

In a special place, the "Be Good Journal" they kept,
    to record her good deeds and rewards that were left.

    She's been such a good girl many times as of late,
        keeping track in her journal helps her motivate.

                She shares with her friends the good things she has done
                    and the "wished for" surprises;
                        the Be Good Fairy's such fun!

Anna Goes to Bed

There was a young girl. Her name was Anna.
She lived on a farm with her papa and nana.

She had many pets: a dog and a cat.
She had a pet pig that was so very fat.

She obeyed her grandparents and did what she was told
except for at bedtime when her behavior was too bold.

One afternoon while milking the cow,
Nana saw bright stardust
and ran home shouting, "Wow!"

She had to tell Papa, and of course Anna too,
the Be Good Fairy's stardust was a beautiful blue.

That night Anna knew that in bed she must be,
and the book she had dreamt of
made her giggle with glee.

To let the fairy know which one was her room,
she hung out her sign: "I've been good," so come soon.

At the break of the day,
Anna ran out to look;
with anticipation she hoped for the new book.

In awe and amazement, what she saw with surprise,
was the biggest book ever.

She couldn't believe its size.

Through the house she went running, waving her prize.
The Be Good Fairy taught: Early to bed...Early to rise!

Addison Misbehaves

Addison's mommy, at the grocery store,
was shopping for dinner when from ceiling to floor
the fairy stardust appeared like a bright shining light,
and she instantly knew who would come the next night.

Later that day she was excited to share
the news the Be Good Fairy had to bear,
"If you'll be good tomorrow at school, don't you see,
you may get a surprise!" Addison lit up with glee.

During lunchtime at school was his biggest flaw,
instead of eating food quietly, he shot peas through his straw!

Mrs. Baker said, "To time-out you go."
A report was sent home so his parents would know.

Mommy said sadly, "The Be Good Fairy might opt,
when passing our house to continue and not stop!"

Addison still hung his "I've Been Good" sign on his door,
in hopes his bad behavior would be ignored.

The next morning he woke and rushed out to find
the Be Good Fairy was surely not blind.

It sees everything, so remember you should,
like Addison learned, Always Be Good!

Jackson Shares

Right in the middle of the big city lights
lived a playful lil' boy who loved to fly kites.

He lived with his mother,
an older sister too,
a brother much younger,
and a kitty named Blue.

On most weekends he spent time with his dad.
They flew kites in the park. What good times they had.

His name was Jackson, and he was so caring,
but his biggest problem was taking turns and not sharing.

When his dad took the subway on Saturday morn,
down came fairy stardust in a bright purple storm.

When he got to the apartment, for Jackson he looked.
He couldn't wait to tell him the route that he took.

Dad told Jackson the lesson to learn,
"The Be Good Fairy is near, so please wait your turn."

When the whole family went out for ice cream that night
he let his sister go first, because he knew that was right.

On the way home he reached into his pocket
and handed his brother his favorite toy rocket.

His dad then said with a smile on his face,
"You've earned a surprise; put your 'Be Good' sign in place."

That night when Jackson went to bed, don't you know,
up went his sign "I've Been Good" sure to show.

When time to awake, he couldn't run fast enough.
What did the fairy bring? What kind of good stuff?

He shot out of his door, after stumbling to unlock it,
and found sitting outside a shiny new rocket!

So rockets he played that day with his brother.
He was excited to get home and tell it all to his mother.

She heard he'd "Been Good," the best of all time.
She said, "Sharing is fun, and taking turns is just fine."

They learned all their lessons,
and the Be Good Fairy helped teach:

"Good deeds will be noticed and are always within reach!"

The End

Now come join us at: TheBeGoodFairy.com

Find us on
Facebook: The Be Good Fairy

20

Find us on
Twitter: @ Be Good Fairy

My Be Good Journal

_____

_____

_____

_____

_____

_____

_____

_____

_____

Name: _____   Date: _____

Draw Your Best Be Good Fairy Below:

~ Use the space provided to draw your best Be Good Fairy. ~

Expert Opinion

by **Caroline Sherril, PhD**

It is human nature to expect good behavior from children. As such, parents tend to take children's good behavior for granted. We often punish the bad but do not acknowledge the good. Good discipline involves two parts: showing children what not to do AND showing children what to do. The Be Good Fairy is a fun and magical way to recognize young children's good behaviors and to give them the positive attention and encouragement they need in order to keep being good.

Dr. Caroline Sherril is a licensed clinical psychologist with a PhD in Clinical Psychology from Vanderbilt University and is a partner at the Behavioral Institute of Atlanta. She specializes in children from two to eight years old and the assessment and treatment of developmental disabilities, childhood behavioral problems, learning disabilities, and ADHD.

The Be Good Fairy.com

Cut Out Your Door Hanger

I've Been Good

~ Kids, ask your parents for help cutting out the door hanger. ~

The Be Good Fairy.com

The Be Good Fairy

Name: _____

From: _____

Date: _____

Note From the Author

by **Missy Wallen-Nichols**

Over the last seven years, I have been putting together stories and examples of families whose lives have been changed by the Be Good Fairy. Becoming a mother later in life, I quickly learned that parenting was more challenging than I had realized. My husband and I wanted a way to discipline our child in a positive and inspiring manner, and a magical entity paved the way to a more peaceful and serene home.

Our family has been touched by the Be Good Fairy in so many wonderful ways. The Be Good Fairy helped discipline and growth become a fun and positive experience for our entire family. We feel compelled to share it with children and families whose lives have not yet been touched by this wonderful force.

I say thank you to my son, Addison, who has been my true inspiration. I have been privileged to see him grow and mature with the help of the Be Good Fairy. Special thanks to Micah Howard. Without him, this book would still be a dream tucked deep in a desk drawer. Deep appreciation to the artist Ben Ballard for his inspired illustrations and to Jake Williams at Lux Studios for his time and expertise in book design and printing. Most of all, I would like to thank the Be Good Fairy for always being there to help and for inspiring me to tell its story. I hope that by writing this book, the door will be opened for parents and children around the world to experience the magic of the Be Good Fairy.